LITTLE MISS
CONTRARY
all in a muddle

Original concept by Roger Hargreaves
Illustrated and written by Adam Hargreaves

MR. MEN   **LITTLE MISS**

MR. MEN™ LITTLE MISS™ © THOIP (a Sanrio company)

Little Miss Contrary all in a muddle © 1998 THOIP (a Sanrio company)
Printed and published under licence from Price Stern Sloan, Inc., Los Angeles.
This edition published in 2013 by Dean, an imprint of Egmont UK Limited,
The Yellow Building, 1 Nicholas Road, London W11 4AN
ISBN 978 0 6035 6891 6
55645/1
Printed in Italy

Now, Little Miss Contrary lives in a place called Muddleland.

In Muddleland, hens live in cow barns, which works.

And cows live in chicken coops, which doesn't work!

Muddleland suits Little Miss Contrary down to the ground, or up to the sky, as they say in Muddleland.

When she goes into the butcher's and asks for apples the butcher gives her a loaf of bread!

Which is what she had wanted all along.

Not so very long ago Little Miss Contrary was having breakfast, at lunchtime, when the telephone rang.

Little Miss Contrary went to the front door, but of course there was no one there.

The phone rang again. She picked it up. The wrong way round. "Goodbye!" she shouted.

Everyone in Muddleland has to shout when they use the phone.

It was Mr Muddle.

Now you would think Mr Muddle also lived in Muddleland, wouldn't you?

But he doesn't.

He wanted to, but got muddled up and bought a house on the coast near Seatown.

However, each year he goes to Muddleland for his holidays and stays with Little Miss Contrary.

"I'd simply hate for you to come and stay. I'll see you last week."

"Hello!" finished Miss Contrary, and hung up.

Little Miss Contrary looked around her.

"This house needs a good autumn-clean," she said to herself.

And, of course, what she meant was that her house needed a good spring-clean.

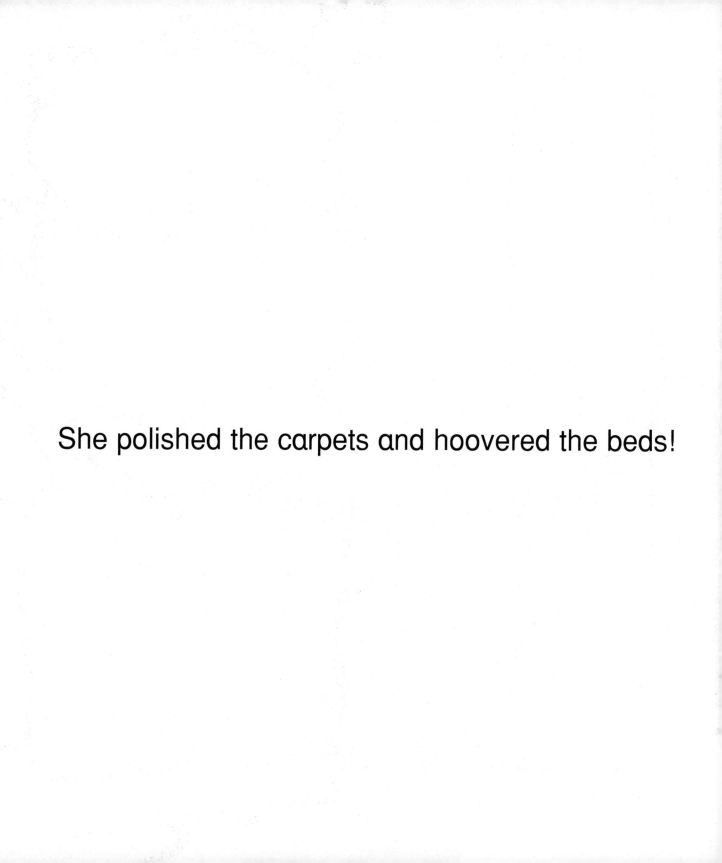

She polished the carpets and hoovered the beds!

And she scrubbed the television and washed the plants!

In the middle of all this scrubbing and polishing and washing, Little Miss Contrary saw a cat.

Little Miss Contrary is terrified of cats.

Well, she isn't called Miss Contrary for nothing, is she?

With an 'EEEEK!' she leapt on to a stool.

Poor Little Miss Contrary.

She was too frightened to get down off the stool.

And there she stayed.

All night long.

The next morning there was a knock at the door.

"Go away!" called Little Miss Contrary, meaning 'come in'.

Luckily it was Mr Muddle on the other side of the door, so in he went.

"Oh, don't help me!" cried Little Miss Contrary. "There's a cat loose in the house!"

Mr Muddle understood completely.
"I don't know what to do," he said, and left.

What he meant was that he did know what to do.

And in no time at all he returned with a mouse.

And the mouse, being a Muddleland mouse, chased the cat out of the house.

Little Miss Contrary made a saucer of tea and she and Mr Muddle settled down for a chat.

A chat that is much too muddling to write down here, and anyway, it's getting late now, and it's time to switch off the light and go to sleep.

Well it isn't really, but that is what Little Miss Contrary would have written if she was writing this story, but luckily she isn't.

You see, Little Miss Contrary gets everything the wrong way round.

She turns her lights off when it gets dark ...

... and turns them on when she goes to bed!

Good morning!